THE SECRET OF
BETE GRISE BAY

A Michigan Lighthouse Adventure

By M. C. Tillson

Illustrated by Lisa T. Bailey

For Micah even now,
to Lisa, Fran, and Lloyd once again,
to my parents, Anne and David, who have always been there
in so many ways,
and to everyone who wanted to hear the rest of the story.

The Secret of Bete Grise Bay
Copyright © 2008 by M. C. Tillson.
All rights reserved.

ISBN 978-0-9764824-2-0

Library of Congress Control Number: 2008900205

Printed in the U.S.A
First printing, October 2008

A LIGHTHOUSE ADVENTURE BOOK
PUBLISHED BY A&M WRITING AND PUBLISHING
SANTA CLARA, CALIFORNIA

CONTENTS

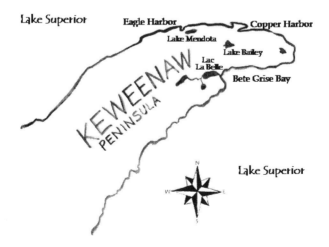

Hi There!

Do you have a minute? There are a couple of things I'd like you to know before you start reading this book.

If this is your first Michigan Lighthouse Adventure book, let me just tell you that Sam and Becky are in the middle of solving a mystery. The story takes place on the Keweenaw Peninsula, a little thumb of land that sticks out into Lake Superior from Michigan's Upper Peninsula. The mystery is about a boy named Tom Adams (who happens to be a ghost) and a witch named Malina who put this curse on Tom:

Hear my voice, oh magic tower,
Take this boy's last drop of power,
Voice and body from him take,
Drown his magic in the lake.

Entwine his gifts in riddles three,
Another's aid the only key.
From my curse now let him cower,
Hear my voice, oh magic tower.

Malina put this curse on Tom because she didn't like him helping the sailors on Lake Superior when they were in trouble. Sam and Becky are trying to help Tom break the curse by solving three riddles, but time is running out and there's still one riddle to solve.

You should know that Sam and Becky and the other characters in this book are not real. This is, after all, a fictional story, and all the characters are made-up people. However, the places I tell you about in this story actually exist on Michigan's magical Upper Peninsula.

Don't Skip the Hard Words

When you read, do you ever skip over words you don't know? Sometimes I do, but most of the time I can figure out what the word means by the other words around it. (That's called **context**.)

But what if the context is not there or doesn't give you the exact meaning? Well, in this book, I've added some definitions for you.

> **CONTEXT**
> (KAHN-tekst)
> The words or sentences around a word that help explain its meaning.

When you see a word written in bold letters (like the word *context* above), look around on the same page for a definition of the word. This will help you understand the story better and will also give you some new words to add to your vocabulary!

7

Check It Out

There are many wonderful books and websites about lighthouses and especially about the lighthouses of the Great Lakes. I've included a list of some of my favorites for you at the end of this book. Be sure to check them out!

Chapter 1
ON THE ROAD AGAIN

"Is everybody here?"

Dad clicked his seatbelt in place and moved the rearview mirror so he could see into the back seat. "If you're not here, raise your hand. Do you see any hands, Alice? No? Then I guess we're all here. OK, let's get going."

"Uh, Dad?" Sam was in the back seat looking a little confused. "Dad, if someone's not here, then how can they raise their hand to show they aren't here?"

"Exactly," said Dad as he started the car. "It works every time." He pulled the car out of the parking lot and started down the road.

Sam and Becky and their mom and dad left the town of Eagle Harbor, Michigan, on the shore of Lake Superior and turned inland. Today they were headed all the way across the Keweenaw Peninsula to **Bete Grise Bay**.

✳ BETE GRISE BAY (bay-de-GREE bay) A sheltered inlet of Lake Superior on the south side of the Keweenaw Peninsula. ("Bete Grise" means "gray beast" in French.)

As Mom and Dad pointed out sights to each other along the gently climbing road, Sam and Becky whispered in the back seat.

"Do you think we'll be able to find the third riddle when we get to Bete Grise Bay?" Sam leaned over so only Becky could hear his question.

"I don't know, Sam," Becky whispered back. "I mean, we don't even know for sure that Bete Grise Bay is where the riddle is!"

"But the waitress said—"

"I know, Sam. I know. She said we'd like Bete Grise Bay."

"Do you still think the waitress is the witch?"

"I do. I mean, she had green eyes and a black cat on her jacket, and we saw her put on those purple sunglasses. But I've been thinking. We know there are two witches, right? The good witch named Marina and the bad witch, Malina, who put the spell on Tom."

"Right..."

"And we both think the waitress was a witch and was telling us to go to Bete Grise Bay, right?"

WILD ✳
GOOSE CHASE
(wild goos chays)
A long, search or quest that produces no answers or results.

"Right..."

"But what if the waitress was Malina, the bad witch? What if she told us to go to Bete Grise Bay to trick us? What if it's a **wild goose chase**?"

"I guess that's possible," said Sam slowly, "but I don't think so. I don't think the waitress was the bad witch. Do you remember how mean Malina was when she turned into six-year old Leena back in Eagle Harbor? Our waitress was really nice, so I think she was Marina, the good witch."

"Well," said Becky, "I hope so. But I still wish we had some way to know if Bete Grise Bay was the right place to go."

Chapter 2
THE LIGHTS OF BETE GRISE BAY

"I saw Henrietta's light last night."

The owner of the Mendota Lighthouse put down the paper he was reading and looked at his wife across the breakfast table. "Was it like the last time?" he asked.

"Yep. It was across the canal, but on the shore—right at the edge of the water."

"Are you sure it wasn't just a **reflection** off the lighthouse?"

> **REFLECTION**
> (re-FLEK-shun)
> A duplication of a light or an image seen on a smooth surface such as water or a mirror.

"You know it wasn't. It was her again. The light moved from the beach over to where the old house used to be and then disappeared—like she went inside and turned out the light."

"Maybe she was tired and went to bed."

"Be serious! You know what this means, don't you?"

"Tell me."

"Every time somebody sees Henrietta's light, it means something's about to happen—not necessarily something bad, but something strange. Something that involves our lighthouse."

"You don't really believe that stuff, do you?"

"Yes I do, and I saw her light again last night."

"But..."

"I'm just saying...something strange is about to happen."

* * * * *

"Hey, Mom, how long does it take to get to the Bete Grise Bay lighthouse?" asked Sam.

"We-ell, Sam, that's actually something I need to talk to you kids about. I never really thought it would matter, but then you got so interested in the lighthouses and said you wanted to go to Bete Grise Bay…. Well, I never put the two together until this morning, and then I remembered."

"Remembered what, Mom?" asked Becky.

"Well…I, uh…I remembered that…ah… well, technically, there is no Bete Grise Bay Lighthouse."

"What?" Sam and Becky looked at each other in surprise.

"Dad, did you know about this?" asked Sam.

"Yes, son, I did," said Dad **gravely**, "and I want to assure you that there is no cause for alarm. It will all work out. It's always darkest before the dawn—"

GRAVELY
(GRAYV-lee)
Very serious or with great concern.

"Dad!" said Sam and Becky together.

"OK, OK," said Dad. "The fact is, your mother likes to stir things up a bit by saying things to get everybody all atwitter. For example, your mother knows good and well that there *is* a lighthouse at Bete Grise Bay—it's just not called the Bete Grise Bay Lighthouse. It's called the Mendota Lighthouse."

"Is this true, Mom?" asked Becky. "Is there a lighthouse at Bete Grise Bay?"

"Well, as a matter of fact, there *is* a lighthouse. It's built on Mendota Point and it marks the entrance to the Mendota Shipping Canal that goes up to Lac La Belle. When the big mining companies brought their copper ore from the mines to Lac La Belle, they needed a better way to get the copper out to Lake Superior. So, they straightened the little canal that was there and made it wider and deeper. They also needed a lighthouse to mark the entrance to the canal, so, in 1869, the United States Government built the Mendota Lighthouse on Bete Grise Bay."

"How far away from this lighthouse is the town of Bete Grise Bay?" asked Becky.

There was a pause, and then Mom said slowly, "Well, uh, technically...."

"Oh, Mom," groaned Sam.

"Technically," continued Mom, "there is no longer a town of Bete Grise Bay. There *was* a town called Bete Grise Bay, but in 1940 there were only ten people living there."

"But the lighthouse they built for the mining companies is still there, right?"

"Well, actually...the government shut it down after just one year because the mining companies weren't producing as much ore, and there weren't as many ships going through the canal. Gold had been discovered in California, and many of the miners left the copper mines and moved west.

✳ SARCASTIC
(SAR-kas-tik)
Saying sharp remarks that can be witty and funny, but also hurtful or mean. Sarcastic remarks sometimes mean the opposite of what they actually say or state an obvious point.

They moved the lighthouse tower and a couple of years later, they tore down the rest of the building."

"OK," said Becky slowly, "let me get this straight. We're going to a town that doesn't exist to see a lighthouse that's been torn down. Is that right?"

"Oh no," said Mom quickly. "It turns out that the big ships needed a lighthouse when they used Bete Grise Bay as a shelter from storms. They rebuilt the lighthouse in 1895."

"Maybe they should have thought of that before they tore it down," said Sam **sarcastically**.

"Well, they decided to rebuild the lighthouse on the same spot—Mendota Point—so they called it the Mendota Lighthouse."

"OK," said Becky patiently, "so we're going to Bete Grise Bay to see the Mendota Lighthouse that marks the beginning of the Mendota Canal to Lac La Belle. Is that right?"

"Exactly," said Mom. "See, Mike I told you they'd understand. It's so simple."

Sam and Becky rolled their eyes at each other as Dad continued down the road toward Bete Grise Bay.

Chapter 3
BEARY PICKING

"Why are we stopping, Dad? This isn't Bete Grise Bay. I don't see any water."

"You're right, Sam," said Dad. "But we're in no hurry. Besides, look—there by the road—blueberries! They grow wild around here and people just pull over to the side of the road and pick 'em. We can pick some for dinner!"

"I don't know, Dad," said Becky looking at Sam, "I think we should get to Bete Grise Bay as soon as we can."

"What's the rush?" asked Dad as he opened the car door. "We don't have any deadlines. We're not meeting anybody that I know of. Come on! We're on vacation! Alice, do we have a bowl or a bag to put the berries in?"

"Here, use this," said Mom handing Dad the junk basket from the car. "I can put all this stuff in a bag for now."

Becky looked at Sam and shook her head. "I guess we're going to pick blueberries," she said.

"Well, Dad may not have a deadline," said Sam, "but we sure do. If we can't find that riddle soon, then Tom will never get his powers back."

"I know," said Becky scooting across the seat to Sam's side of the car. "And he'll lose his voice and be invisible again."

"Not only do we have to find the riddle, but we have to solve it before the next full moon—and that's tomorrow night! Come on, Becky. Let's go help Dad pick blueberries so we can get going again."

Sam jumped out of the car and almost fell into the drainage ditch at the side of the road.

"Whoops! Watch that first step there, Sam," Dad called from the blueberry patch where he was standing. "It's a 'berry' long one."

"Thanks, Dad. Thanks for the 'berry' late warning."

"Where *are* the berries, Dad?" Becky stood beside the car looking at the patches of green in front of her. She took a couple of steps toward the leaves and bent down. "All I can see are—oh, wow! Sam, look at all the berries! You have to look under the leaves a bit and then—wow! They're so small that it's hard to see them, but there are tons of them here!"

Becky popped a couple of the little blue berries into her mouth. "YUM! They're *so* good. They're really sweet. Taste some, Sam."

"Uh alledy ab sum," said Sam with his mouth packed full of the sweet little berries.

"Look at all of them over there," said Becky. "Come on, Sam. Let's go pick those."

Becky led Sam to a patch of blueberries a little ways from the car and they both started picking the tiny berries. "There must be a million of them," she said to Sam. "Maybe we can pick enough to make a pie tonight!"

For the next two nights, Mom, Dad, Sam, and Becky were spending the night in a cabin right on the western shore of Bete Grise Bay. Dad's brother Joe owned the cabin, but he was away for the summer. When Dad called Uncle Joe and told him they had changed their plans and wanted to visit Bete Grise Bay, Joe offered to let them stay at his little house.

Becky heard something moving in the bushes right behind her. "Go find your own berries, Sam! These are mine." Sam didn't say anything, but the rustling noise got louder. "Did you hear me, Sam? Go find another patch to pick."

"Wha'dju say, Becky?" Becky jerked her head up and saw Sam standing in a patch of blueberries in front of her.

But wait…if Sam was over there, then who was making the noise behind her?

Becky turned around slowly and saw something black and furry in the bushes. She looked closer and saw two little eyes looking back at her. It was a furry, little, black…bear!

25

Aunt Isabel often told them stories about the black bears that were all over the Keweenaw Peninsula. The bears were usually after food, not people, but where there was a baby bear, there was sure to be a mama bear close by. And there were very few things scarier than a mama bear protecting her cub.

Becky backed slowly away from the little bear and tiptoed as quietly as she could toward the car. Sam was picking berries with his back to her. "Sam!" hissed Becky, "Sam! Bear!"

Sam didn't look up. He was too busy picking blueberries. "I know you've got berries, Becky. I've got a bunch too. This was a good patch."

"No, Sam. BEAR!"

"What?"

"Shhh! Be quiet! There's a baby bear over there in the bushes. No, Sam, don't!" whispered Becky as Sam stood up and turned around. "We've got to get back to the car. The mama bear is probably close by." Sam grabbed his bag of blueberries and they took off for the car.

"Dad! Mom!" Sam whispered loudly, "Black bear!"

Mom and Dad were busy picking berries on the other side of the car. "Actually, Sam," said Dad in a loud voice, "blackberries aren't ripe until a little later in the season. These blueberries are the first to ripen. Next come the thimbleberries and then…"

"What's wrong with your throat, Sam?" called Mom. "Are you catching a cold?"

"Mom! Dad!" yelled Becky. "There's a black bear over here!"

"What?" Mom and Dad came rushing out from behind the car. "Where?"

"Over there! Look!" Becky pointed back to the patch of berries where she had seen the little bear. Only now, instead of one bear, there were two little heads sticking up out of the blueberry patch.

"OK," said Mom, "everybody in the car and I MEAN NOW!"

Four doors slammed shut as Sam, Becky, Mom, and Dad jumped into the car. While Dad put on his seatbelt and started the car, Sam and Becky turned around to watch the little bears who were now wrestling with each other in the berry patch.

"They're in big trouble now," said Sam. He pointed to the woods near the berry patch where they saw a big mama bear **shamble** over to the roly-poly cubs.

> **SHAMBLE**
> (SHAM-bull)
> Walk slowly and clumsily, dragging your feet.

Dad pulled the car back onto the road and, in the back seat, Becky spoke softly to Sam. "Did you get a good look at the first bear cub, Sam? It had green eyes! I don't know about the second one, but the first one had bright green eyes!"

Sam's mouth dropped open and he turned around quickly to catch a glimpse of the baby bears. But the mama bear and the two bear cubs had already moved on to eat blueberries somewhere else.

Chapter 4
WITCH WAY TO BETE GRISE BAY?

"So, how much farther, Dad?"

"We should be there pretty soon. The road signs are pretty good so all we need to do is…" Dad slowed the car and pointed to a sign at the side of the road. "Until now, that is. I'm going to need some time to figure this one out."

Sam and Becky and Mom looked at the sign by the side of the road. It was supposed to explain to drivers about the road ahead, but it was very confusing. One part of the sign had an arrow that went straight and then made a right turn. The other part started with a left turn and then went straight.

"OK," said Dad, "I think we need to go right. Or maybe we need to go left. Or maybe we need to go left and straight at the same time—you know, lefraight. Or maybe we just need to make an O-turn."

"An O-turn, Mike? What are you talking about?"

"Well, I figure that I probably need to go right and straight, or else go straight and then left. But that's probably not right, so I'll make a U-turn, and then I'll probably make another U-turn which works out to be an O-turn." He sighed, "You know, if we have too many more signs like this one, we'll end up back in Eagle Harbor and we'll never make it to Bete Grise Bay."

"It *is* confusing," said Mom, "but I think we should go left and then straight. If we go straight first, we'll end up in the town of Lac La Bell."

"OK, leftraight it is. You know, I don't think we're the only ones who get a little confused. Look at all those mailboxes! I think most of these folks have no idea where they live!"

"Oh, look at the little kitty-cat sitting on that last mailbox," said Mom. "She's just sitting there watching us. She's trying to figure out which way we're going too."

"Well, I hope this way meets with her approval," said Dad.

Sam and Becky turned around to look back at the mailboxes. A sleek, black cat sat on the last mailbox calmly staring after them.

"Sam, look! Did you see—"

"I know, Becky. That cat had a purple collar, didn't it?"

"You know, kids," said Dad from the front seat, "I'm not really sure where we are, but that's OK. One of the things I like most about driving on the Upper Peninsula is that you're always exploring and seeing something new. Everything is a surprise—I love that."

"Hey, Dad…" said Sam.

"Yep," continued Dad, "I really like driving by the seat of our pants, by the skin of our teeth, going wherever the road takes us…"

"Dad!" Sam said a little louder.

"Yes sir, there's nothing like throwing your cares to the wind and seizing the day. I think I could drive forever if—"

"DAD!"

"What, Sam? Don't surprise me like that! You know I hate that! What is it?"

"Dad, we're here!"

Chapter 5
IN SEARCH OF THE GRAY BEAST

Dad parked the car by the side of the road and everyone got out to look around. The sparkling blue waters of Bete Grise Bay stretched out before them, ending at the fuzzy, blue-purple line in the distance that was still Lake Superior.

"Bete Grise Bay. In French that means the bay of the gray beast," said Dad.

"A lot of this area was settled by French Canadians," said Mom, "so there are a lot of French names like Lac La Belle and Bete Grise Bay. I wonder why they call it the gray beast?"

"Maybe the gray beast is the fog," said Dad, "although that's hard to imagine on a day like today."

"Maybe there's actually a gray beast that lives in the bay," said Sam. "You know, like the **Loch Ness Monster**."

Loch Ness Monster (lock nes MON-str) The mythical sea creature that lives in a lake (called Loch Ness) in Scotland. The Loch Ness monster is nicknamed "Nessie."

"I guess we'll just have to keep our eyes open for a gray beast." said Becky.

"Among other things," said Sam under his breath.

"This really is beautiful," said Mom. "It seems like everywhere else on the Keweenaw Peninsula the shoreline is covered with rocks—big ones, small ones, but lots and lots of rocks. But here…well, just look at the sand. Look how white it is. Even the water is a different color—more blue, I think."

"Yep," said Dad stretching his arms above his head and looking around. "Look at that. Miles of sandy beach and even some trees to break the wind. If you were a ship captain running in front of a storm, Bete Grise Bay would look pretty good to you. Yes sir, a lot of ships have weathered a lot of storms here.

"Of course, storms weren't the only thing that threatened the ships. The crew of the *Langham* outran a storm, but then ended up watching as their ship was destroyed by fire. I don't think they ever figured out what happened, but the *Langham* sank right over there." Dad pointed toward the western shore of the bay.

"Look," said Mom, "there's the lighthouse. Of course, since somebody actually lives there, we can't just pop in for a visit, but we can still get a great picture for the book.

"Sam, why don't you and Becky take the camera and walk up the beach. You can get a picture of the lighthouse and stretch your legs. Dad and I are going to put a blanket on the sand right here. I might even take a little nap. Mike, would you pass me the sunscreen, please?"

"Great idea, Alice! I'm always up for a nap. Are you sure you kids don't want to join us? Nothing like a nice nap to get you going on a beautiful day like this."

"No thanks, Dad," said Sam. "I think we're going to explore." As he and Becky started off down the beach, he continued in a low grumble, "…although I don't know what we're going to explore since there's nothing here and even the lighthouse is off limits."

"Oh, come on, Sam," said Becky. "That's not fair. There *is* a lighthouse—a really nice one. I know it's not called the Bete Grise Bay Lighthouse and I know that it's not open to the public and I know that we can't get to it because of the canal to Lac La Belle—"

"If you're trying to make me feel better, Becky, you're doing a terrible job."

"Wow, you really are grumpy," said Becky.

It really was a beautiful day. The water—clear, smooth, and bright royal blue—sparkled in the sunlight. Out in the middle of the bay, a **kayak** moved slowly across the water. Below their feet, the white sand stretched for miles; nothing interrupted it except the occasional lazy wave lapping at the shore.

KAYAK ✳
(KI-yak)
A portable boat modeled after the covered canoes used by Eskimos.

But Sam, still grumbling, noticed none of it. "No town. No lighthouse. No people. How are we going to find a riddle and help Tom? This is crazy. What are we supposed to do— dig in the sand for a buried clue? If we don't find that third riddle before the full moon—"

"And solve it," added Becky.

"And solve it," agreed Sam, "Tom will disappear forever."

Chapter 6
THE SONG OF THE SAND

As Sam grumbled to himself, he walked faster and faster. He didn't notice that Becky was falling behind and was now standing perfectly still. She was looking at the sand with her head cocked to one side.

"Sam, do you hear that?"

"Hear what?" grumbled Sam. "The only thing I hear is the sound of us not getting any closer to a riddle. Tom is so sure we can help him—I wish I were that sure."

"Listen, Sam."

Sam stopped and looked at Becky with a question on his face.

"It's gone now," she said as she hurried toward him. "I don't hear anything but…"

"Wait, Becky! I do hear it. It sounds like…like barking…no, it sounds like somebody singing."

Becky stopped and the sound stopped too.

"Walk," commanded Sam.

Becky took a few steps on the sand and they both heard a noise that sounded like the sharp bark of a very small dog. Becky walked faster and the noise changed. She caught up with Sam and they both walked quickly toward the lighthouse. As they did, they heard the sand singing a strange, sad song beneath their feet.

"Do you hear it, Sam?"

"Yeah, I do. It's only when you walk. When you start, every step sounds like a dog barking, but when you walk fast, it sounds more like music—a really sad song. It's weird."

"Maybe it's a clue," said Becky hopefully.

"Oh yeah, that'd be great. A clue where we have to sing a weird song or bark like a dog. Terrific."

By now Sam and Becky had reached the edge of the canal to Lac La Belle. The wall that marked the canal was too tall to see over and was surrounded by big, mean-looking rocks and even bigger signs that said "No Trespassing."

"So now what?" said Sam. "We can't get any closer to the lighthouse because the canal cuts us off. We can't go inside the lighthouse because somebody lives there. What are we going to do?"

"What are we going to do about what?"

"Gee, Becky, aren't you listening to me?"

"I was listening, Sam, but I wasn't talking. I didn't say anything."

Sam turned around and looked down the beach. He saw the footprints he had made in the sand, he saw Becky's footprints, and he saw…a third set of footprints!

Sam looked over his shoulder to where the footprints ended. "Tom," he said in a very loud whisper, "Tom, is that you?"

"Well, who else would it be?" came the whispered reply. "Do you have a *lot* of invisible friends? And why are we whispering?" With a chuckle, Tom Adams appeared on the beach right in front of them.

"Wow! It's good to see you guys!" said Tom. "I wasn't sure you'd make it here, but I hoped you would."

"It's good to see you too, Tom! But why are you smiling? Don't you know what happens tomorrow night?" Sam still had a frown on his face.

"Yeah, I know. Tomorrow is the full moon, but you guys are here today and I just know you're going to help me. So, by tomorrow night I'll be my old self again. Just thinking about it makes me smile."

"I hope you're right," said Sam shaking his head, "but to be honest, right now we don't have a clue about what to do."

"I should go," whispered Tom and he pointed down the beach.

Sam looked around and saw a lady chasing a dog along the beach and coming toward them. He turned back to Tom who was fading quickly.

"I sure hope we figure out something before you come back."

"I know you will," answered Tom, his voice drifting out across the water as his ghostly body disappeared.

"I don't know," muttered Sam, "but I hope you're right."

Chapter 7
DOG-GONE FUNNY

"Spotty! Here boy!"

Sam and Becky didn't pay much attention to the lady chasing the dog. After Tom disappeared, Becky sat down and started drawing in the sand. Sam joined her and soon the drawing changed into serious sandcastle building.

As they worked, Sam and Becky talked about the third riddle.

"OK," said Becky for what must have been the tenth time, "let's review what we know about the third riddle. We know that Tom thinks the riddle is here at Bete Grise Bay. We also know that the waitress at the restaurant—who we think is the good witch, Marina—told us we'd like Bete Grise Bay and encouraged us to come here. So that's good."

"OK," said Sam, "but what about the bear cub? And the cat on the mailbox?"

"I think they were signs that we're in the right place," said Becky.

"Maybe..." said Sam.

"We just need to remember whether the waitress gave us any clues. What did she say while we were there?"

"Well, she said that the beaches at Bete Grise Bay were nice and sandy...no, that was the lady at the cash register. Let me think. The waitress said that the blueberry syrup was good on the thimbleberry pancakes and she suggested we try the chicken apple sausage and she said it was cool that we were going to Bete Grise Bay and she wished us good luck—which I really didn't understand."

"Right," said Becky, her eyes growing wide with excitement, "but she also said there was a lot to see if you look in the right spot…no, wait that's not what she said. She said 'There's a lot to see if you find the right spot.' That's it! I think she was giving us a clue."

"Well, if that's the only clue we've got, then we're in a lot of trouble. Finding the right spot sounds like a treasure hunt. Maybe we should just look around for a great big X on the beach and then we'll dig for a buried treasure chest and find the riddle inside."

"Oh come on, Sam. I know it's not much of a clue, but it's all we've got. And I do think that it tells us that Bete Grise Bay is the right place."

"But finding the right spot…I mean, what are we supposed to do with that?"

Before Becky had a chance to answer, she, Sam, and the sandcastle were attacked by a barking, snuffling, wet ball of fur.

"Oh, yuck!" shouted Sam as the ball of fur took that particular moment to shake cold water and sand all over him. "What *is* that?"

"It's a dogff!" Becky's reply was cut short by a mouth full of sand.

"Naughty dog!" cried a voice from down the beach. "Naughty dog! No! Come here!"

"It *is* a dog," said Becky spitting sand out of her mouth. "It's wagging…and it's putting its paw out to shake. Look, Sam, isn't that cute? He wants to shake."

"He's already done enough shaking—all over me!" Sam was now shaking *his* head trying to get the sand out of his hair.

"He's pretty dirty," agreed Becky taking the dog's paw and giving it a little shake.

"Well, he's a lot cleaner that he used to be," Sam said. He looked at his t-shirt and shorts that were now soaking wet and covered with mud, sand, and paw prints.

"But just look at how cute he is, Sam. He's still just a puppy."

At their feet, being as good as gold, sat a dirty, medium-sized, white dog with black and brown spots. He was panting heavily and his tongue was hanging out to one side after his surprise attack on the sandcastle. His dark brown eyes twinkled as if he knew a secret he wanted to share.

"Oh, I am so sorry! What a naughty dog you are!" A lady holding an empty leash stumbled up to Sam and Becky and shook her finger at the little dog. "He didn't hurt you, did he? He loves people and he loves the beach, and when there are people on the beach...well, he's just uncontrollable. As soon as I saw you up here building a...oh, no! Look what he did to your sandcastle. I *am* sorry."

"It's OK," said Sam. "We were just playing around. He didn't know."

"He's so cute," said Becky, "and polite—at least when there are no sandcastles to attack. What's his name?"

"Well," said the lady, "his official name is Steven Patrick Oliver, the Third, but mostly we just call him Spot. Get it? S-P-O-T, Spot! Although, if my sister is around, we have a problem. She has a cat whose name is also Spot, so when they visit, we call her cat Left Spot and this troublemaker right here we call Right Spot."

"Well, Sam," said Becky slowly, "call me crazy, but I think we just found the right spot."

Chapter 8
SEEING SPOTS

The lady sank slowly down to the warm sand and breathed a deep sigh. "Ohhh, that's better." Spot, exhausted from his war with the sandcastle, flopped at her feet and promptly went to sleep.

"That dog is going to be the end of me. If he wasn't such a sweetheart—at least most of the time—I wouldn't keep him. But he's so enthusiastic and such good company, and he loves the beach. It's fun to take him along on my walks."

"He *is* very...uh...energetic," agreed Sam crouching down beside Spot and rubbing his silky ears. "Does he dig a lot? Has he ever discovered a treasure chest?"

Becky rolled her eyes as the lady laughed. "No," said the lady, "he's never discovered a treasure chest, but he did discover the daffodil bulbs I planted last fall. Dug them up and brought them up to the house one by one. I had planted over fifty bulbs. I didn't figure out what was going on until it was too late and all fifty bulbs were piled—quite neatly—on my front porch."

Sam and Becky laughed as the woman shook her head. "I decided it was his way of bringing me flowers—just a little early! And then I decided to plant the bulbs in pots instead. So are you from around here or are you visiting?"

"We're visiting," said Becky. "Our mom and dad are writing a book about lighthouses in Michigan. They are back there on the beach taking a nap."

"Well, uh…actually, I don't think they are napping anymore," said the woman. "I think Spot took care of that when I was chasing him. I hope they aren't mad."

"I'm sure they're fine," said Becky squinting to look down the beach. She saw Mom shaking sand out of her hair and Dad vigorously shaking out the blanket where only minutes before he had been sleeping peacefully. "They love dogs…at least they used to."

"So, your mom and dad are writing a book about lighthouses? That's fascinating. I love lighthouses.

> **FIGURINE**
> (fig-u-REEN)
> A small molded or carved statue.

I collect them—well, not the actual lighthouses, of course, but little **figurines** and magnets and earrings, see?" She pulled her hair back and waggled her head at Sam and Becky.

"This one is Eagle Harbor lighthouse and this is the lighthouse at Copper Harbor. I like to wear different ones at the same time.

"Yesterday, a friend of mine gave me a little **medallion** that—oh, that's right! I was going to put it on Spot's collar and I forgot. It's supposed to be good luck. Well, I'll just put it on him when we get home. It's really a nice medallion. It has the Mendota Lighthouse on one side and on the other side there's some writing. A poem maybe. It was a little hard to read. Anyway, I figured that if anybody could use some good luck, it's Spot."

MEDALLION
(mi-DAL-yun)
A large medal.

Hearing his name, Spot jumped to his feet. He was totally refreshed from his catnap and ready to play He wagged his tail and barked at Sam. When Sam didn't move, Spot ran around in a circle chasing his tail until he got so dizzy he fell down in a heap—but with his tail finally caught in his mouth.

Spot looked up at Sam who was laughing so hard his face was red. Seeing this as some sort of signal, Spot crouched down with his bottom up in the air, and started barking at Sam again.

"Come here, Spot," said Becky in a low soothing voice. But Spot whipped around and turned his fierce barking on her. With his bottom in the air and his head between his front paws, Spot gave a deep, scary bark, but it was a little hard to take him seriously because his tail was wagging wildly.

Becky called his name again, and Spot promptly **surrendered.** He flopped down, turned over on his back, and waited for someone to scratch his belly.

SURRENDER
(sir-REN-dur)
Give up and turn yourself in to the other side.

61

Becky laughed, but gently scratched Spot's tummy. His eyes closed in delight and soon he was making little puppy snoring noises.

"Is there any way we could see the medallion that your friend gave to you?" asked Becky. "Sam and I like lighthouses too."

"Are you staying in the area?" asked the lady.

"We're staying in our uncle's cabin for a couple of days. Its over on the other side of the bay."

"Well, I walk with Spot on the beach every morning around 6:30. You could see the medallion then if you want. I'm going to put it on him when I get home. Maybe Spot's luck will improve. Shall I look for you tomorrow?"

"Oh yes!" said Sam and Becky together. "We'll see you then."

"Great! Come on, Spot. It's time to go."

And as Sam and Becky watched, Spot—with the end of his leash in his mouth— walked himself down the beach, with his owner following closely behind.

Chapter 9
SPIT SPOT

"But you don't even like dogs. Why do you want to take him for a walk?" Marina sat on the floor of the kitchen rubbing behind Spot's ears as she looked up at her sister.

"That's not true! I love dogs. And they love me. Watch. Here, Spot. Come here, Spotty. Come here, sweetie."

Marina watched as her sister, Malina, whistled and called and patted her knees. Spot watched too. He sat quietly (unusual for him) cocking his head from one side to the other, but never moving from Marina's side.

"You're holding him," protested her sister. "He'll never come to me if you're holding him."

Marina showed the palms of both her hands. "He just knows you're a cat person, Leena. He probably thinks you're calling your kitty."

"Oh fine, then. Can I take him with me on my walk anyway? He's good protection."

Marina burst into laughter. "Yeah, if you run into any trouble he can bark at it and chase his tail. Yessiree, he's quite the guard dog."

Malina looked at Marina, not smiling at her sister's jokes. "Are you finished making fun of me yet? I'd like to go for my walk and I'd like to take Spot with me."

"Good grief, Malina. Spot is only six months old—he's still a puppy—and you're a witch. Why do you need him to protect you?"

"You only call me 'Malina' when you're angry at me," said Malina. "OK, maybe I don't need Spot for protection. Maybe I just wanted to help. I know he needs to go for a walk and I know how busy you are right now. Can't a person do something nice?"

Malina turned away from her sister. "Besides, I have a lot I need to think about right now and Spot is good company. He keeps me from being lonely." She sighed. "But, if you don't trust me with your dog, then just say so. I can certainly go for a walk...all by myself...in the dark."

Marina felt a twinge of shame. "Well, of course, you can take him with you, Leena. He always loves to go for a walk. I'm sorry. I never realized how much this meant to you."

She clipped Spot's red leash to his collar and handed the other end to her sister. "Just be careful. He's not very good at walking on the leash yet and he'll try to get loose. Hey, did you see this medallion? I just put it on Spot's collar. It has a picture of the Mendota Lighthouse on it. It's supposed to be good luck. "

"Oh, I hadn't noticed. That's nice," said Malina pulling on her jacket. "Come on, Spot."

"Don't be too long," Marina called after them. "Dinner will be ready soon."

* * * * * * *

Once she and Spot were outside, Malina pulled Spot toward the beach.

"Medallion? Oh no, I didn't notice the medallion, Marina. It's perfectly lovely!" she said, sarcastically mimicking Marina's sweet voice. "It's only the medallion that can remove the curse from Tom and bring my whole plan crashing down. Of *course* I noticed the medallion, you fool. Why do you think I insisted on taking this horrible dog for a walk? Come on, dog."

The moon was just beginning to rise over the tip of the Keweenaw Peninsula and Bete Grise Bay, and even though the sky was still light with the evening glow of summer in the North, a few stars were starting to appear. But Malina paid no attention to any of it. As soon as they got to the beach, she walked faster. Her quick steps made the sand bark, and Spot—both alarmed and excited—ran around in circles tangling up Malina in his leash.

As Malina tried to untangle her legs from the leash, she yelled at Spot. "Stop it, Spot! Come here!"

In response, Spot crouched down, put his bottom up in the air, and barked loudly. When Malina grabbed at the dog and his collar, Spot dodged her hand. He ran around behind her and barked again. She turned and grabbed at him again. This time she caught a handful of fur, but Spot wiggled free and ran down the beach dragging the red leash behind him. Every few yards he stopped and turned around to make sure Malina was following.

"Come back here, Spot! Come on, Spot. Here, Spotty. Come to Auntie Leena," she said in a high voice and then suddenly in an angry screech, "Bad dog! Bad dog. Get back here, you worthless animal."

But Spot paid no attention. He ran down the beach a little ways and then flopped down on the sand. Three seconds later he jumped up and trotted to the edge of the water. He sniffed at the water and then started digging furiously. He was so busy exploring and digging that he never even heard Malina come up behind him.

"OK, you little mutt," said Malina, grabbing Spot by the **scruff** of the neck. "You've had your fun—now it's my turn. Let me have that medallion."

SCRUFF
(skruf)
The back of the neck.

While Spot struggled to get away, Malina pulled the medallion off his collar. As soon as she had it in her hand, she dropped Spot back on the sand.

"At last," she whispered to herself. "They'll never find it now. And, with a wicked laugh, Malina threw the medallion far, far, far into the middle of Bete Grise Bay.

The medallion shone bright for a moment as it flew through the air and landed with a small splash in the waters that knew so many secrets.

"Have your friends find *that*, Tom Adams," said Malina, smiling to herself. Then she started back to the house where her sister was making dinner.

Spot trotted quietly beside her, the red leash trailing in the sand behind them.

Chapter 10
GOOD MORNING?

The next morning, Sam and Becky woke up a little before six o'clock. Even though it was early, the sun was already up in the sky. The days were longer on the Keweenaw in the summer: The sun didn't set until after nine o'clock at night and sunrise was an early five o'clock in the morning.

Uncle Joe's cabin had a big room with both a kitchen and living room in it. There was also a bedroom, a bathroom, and a **loft** where Sam and Becky slept.

LOFT
(lawft)
An upper room or floor.

Sam tiptoed into Mom and Dad's bedroom where their parents were still asleep. Dad's snoring made conversation difficult, so Sam bent over his mother.

"Mom," he whispered in her ear, "Becky and I are going for a walk on the beach. Is that OK?"

"Yes, dear," murmured Mom sleepily. "Goodnight, Sam."

"No, Mom, we're not going to bed. We're up, and we're going for a walk on the beach, OK?"

"Sleep tight, dear." Mom turned on her side and put a pillow over her head.

"I give up," said Sam.

"We'll just leave a note," said Becky, "but come on. It's getting late."

A few minutes later, Sam and Becky ran down the path that led to the beach at Bete Grise Bay. Before they even saw Spot, they heard him barking. When they reached the shore, they saw him chasing a flock of seagulls. It seemed like the birds were teasing Spot. They strolled along the sand until Spot almost caught them, and then, at the last minute, they flew away. Spot tried several times to catch a bird, but finally just plopped down on the sand with a confused look on his face.

"Come on, Sam. Let's go check out that medallion," said Becky. She waved to the lady following Spot on the beach.

"Good morning!" the lady called to Sam and Becky. "How are you this fine summer morning?"

"A little sleepy," said Sam, "but ready to see Spot's good-luck medallion."

"Well, you'll have to catch him first. I put it on him the minute we got home yesterday and he's been prancing around with it ever since. You'd think it was the crown of England. I told Captain Pete that…"

"Captain Pete!" interrupted Becky. "Do you know Captain Pete?"

"Oh my, yes! Captain Pete and I go way back. He's the friend I told you about. The one that gave me the medallion. How do you know the captain?"

"We met him on our visit to Copper Harbor," said Sam. "He took us out to the lighthouse and was the first one to tell us about—"

"—to tell us about Eagle Harbor and the cool lighthouse there." Becky interrupted Sam with a shake of her head and a quick frown.

"Captain Pete certainly does love lighthouses. When the Mendota Lighthouse came up for sale, I was sure Captain Pete would buy it. But, I guess it was just too expensive for an old sea captain to afford.

"You know, he'll be bringing a group of divers over from Copper Harbor this morning. They're exploring the ship that burned and sank in the bay—the *Langham*."

"We've heard a lot about that shipwreck," said Becky. "Where exactly did it sink?"

BUOYS
(BOO-eez)
To keep something afloat by attaching it to a floating object that is anchored to the bottom of a lake or channel.

"Over there, right off shore." The lady pointed to the west. "The hull and the engine and things like the rudder, propellers, and anchors are still down there. The Keweenaw Underwater Preserve **buoys** the wreck during the summer months, so it's a great wreck to explore.

By this time, Spot had found a place on the sand between Sam and Becky with his head resting on top of Becky's shoes. As she bent down to scratch Spot's ears, she looked at his collar. She pulled it round and round, but saw no medallion.

"Where's the medallion?" she asked. "I don't see it on his collar. There's a dog tag with his name on it, but that's all."

"What?" cried the lady. "It was there yesterday. Oh no, don't tell me we've lost it! Oh Spot, what happened?" She squatted down beside the little dog to look at his collar.

"Let me think…the last time I saw it was when I put the leash on him yesterday for my sister to take him for a walk. I told you she was visiting, didn't I? With her cat. I guess cats don't take walks because she kept begging to take Spot for a walk even though she usually has nothing to do with him." She leaned over to whisper to Sam and Becky, "My sister doesn't even like dogs."

"Oh, this is awful!" The lady stood up quickly. "Maybe it fell off when they went for a walk. I'll start looking for it right away. Captain

Pete is going to be terribly disappointed. I can't believe it's gone."

The lady walked off down the beach muttering to herself and looking from side to side searching the sand for the medallion. Spot followed, sniffing the ground like a **bloodhound** tracking a scent.

BLOOD-HOUND
(BLUD-hownd)
A special breed of dog used to find people and animals by following their scent.

"I can't believe it," said Becky. "We were so close. That's got to be the third riddle, and now it's gone."

Sam stared after the lady and Spot for a few minutes. "Hey, Becky, did you see what color eyes the lady had?" He nodded his head toward Spot's owner.

"I don't know," said Becky watching Spot and the lady walk down the beach still looking for the medallion. "I never really saw her eyes—she never took off her sunglasses..." Becky swallowed hard and looked over at Sam. "Sam, I'm not sure, but I think the frames for those sunglasses she was wearing were a really, really dark..."

"Purple," finished Sam. "You're right. She was wearing purple sunglasses."

Chapter 11
ON THE BAY

When Sam and Becky returned to the house, they found Mom and Dad already up and dressed.

"Kayaks!" shouted Dad as he saw Sam and Becky.

"Kids," replied Sam in an equally loud voice.

"Kids in kayaks," responded Dad.

"Cool kids in kayaks off the Keweenaw," ventured Becky.

"OK, OK!" said Mom. "Before this cute little game gets out of hand, you should know that your

Uncle Joe has two **tandem kayaks** we can use. He called last night to tell us where they were, and he also predicted that your father would fall in the lake if we used them."

TANDEM
KAYAK
(TAN-dum
KI-yak)
A kayak with seats
for two people.

"He obviously doesn't know that he's challenging the kayak king," said Dad appearing at the door with four life vests in his arms. "So can we go now? Can we, huh? Pleeease?"

"Mike! Give them a chance to catch their breath. Did you two have a nice walk?"

"Not as nice as it should have been," replied Sam.

"It was nice," said Becky. "We saw the little dog from yesterday again."

"Well, grab a snack and get your life vest. Dad and I already carried the kayaks to the water. If we don't hurry up, he's going to leave without us."

Thirty minutes later, Sam, Becky, Mom, and Dad were enjoying the late morning on Bete Grise Bay. Soon after they left the shore, they spotted a boat with divers who were jumping one by one into the water.

"I bet that's the group that Captain Pete brought out from Copper Harbor," said Becky. "Dad, can we go over and say hello?"

"Sure," said Dad. "You and Sam go ahead. Mom and I will...uh...be right behind you."

"Ahoy there, you **landlubbers**," called Captain Pete across the water.

LAND-LUBBER (LAND-lub-burr) A slang word for "land lover"—someone who spends more time on land than on the water.

"Ahoy yourself, Captain Pete!" called back Sam.

"You two are looking pretty good in that kayak. Is this your first time out?"

"It's our first time on Lake Superior, but we go kayaking a lot in California. Mom and Dad too. See them? They sometimes have trouble because they can't decide which one of them is the captain."

"We never have that problem, do we Sam?"

"No, Becky, we don't," said Sam with just a tiny bit of sarcasm. "You're always the captain because you're older, and you always get to sit in the back because you're taller,"

"Well, don't worry, son," said Captain Pete. "It won't always be that way." Then, after looking at Becky's confused face, he quickly explained. "What I mean to say is that Becky will always be older than you, but I expect in a few more years you might outrank her in the tallness department."

"I'll still be captain, though," said Becky.

"Maybe," said Sam."

"Ahoy there, Captain," called Dad as he and Mom paddled up alongside the boat.

"Good day to you and the missus, sir. It's a fine day for being on the water."

"Yes, it is," said Dad. "Looks like it's a fine day for being under the water too."

"Yes, sir. I brought these divers around from Copper Harbor to see the *Langham*. Told them it was my favorite shipwreck to visit."

"Why is that, Captain Pete?" asked Mom.

"Well, it's an easy outing for the new divers, but I've also got a personal connection. You see, my grandfather was part of the crew on the day the *Langham* burned and sank."

"You never told us that, Captain Pete," said Becky.

"Yep. If he and the other sailors hadn't gotten off when they did…well I might not be standing here today."

"Did your grandfather know Tom?" asked Sam.

"Who's Tom?" asked Dad.

"Oh, that's just the name of the ship before they changed it to the *Langham*," said Becky giving Sam a not-so-gentle thwack on the back. "I guess Sam was asking how well Captain Pete's grandfather knew the ship. Was your grandfather the captain of the *Langham*, Captain Pete?"

"Oh, no," said Captain Pete. "Grandpa Dave was pretty young when he was on the *Langham*— only 17 years old. He didn't become a captain until about ten years later. His son, Tom, who was my father, was five years old at the time."

"That's an interesting coincidence," said Mom. "Your father had the same first name as the original *Langham*."

"Yes, ma'am. My Grandpa Dave must'a told me the story of the *Langham* about a hundred times. It made a real impression on him. I guess you never forget a thing like that."

"Well, it's been good to see you, Captain," said Dad with a salute. "We're headed up along the shore here. Alice wants to get a picture of the lighthouse from the water."

"Dad, do you mind if Sam and I stay here and talk to Captain Pete? We'll catch up with you in a little bit."

"I'll keep my eye on them," said Captain Pete. "They might like to see the divers come up. They've been down there for a while, so they should be coming up for a break soon."

"That's OK with me," said Dad. "Alice?"

"That's fine as long as you two are careful and remember all the water safety rules."

"All right, Alice," said Dad, "let's go. Right paddle, ho."

"But I was going to go around this way, dear," said Mom, paddling on her left side.

"But Alice, the lighthouse is over there, so let's use the right paddle."

"But dear…"

Mom and Dad's voices faded into the breeze as their kayak went forward—on a zig-zag path—toward the lighthouse.

"I guess they'll figure it out eventually," said Becky looking after them. "I think it'll be pretty easy to catch up with them."

"So, Captain Pete," said Sam, "it's no coincidence that your father's name is Tom, is it? You grandfather knew Tom Adams, didn't he?"

"You're right, Sam," said Captain Pete, "my grandfather was Tom's friend on the *Langham*."

Chapter 12
GRANDPA DAVE'S STORY

Captain Pete helped Sam and Becky tie the kayak to the diving boat and scramble aboard.

"When Tom Adams stowed away on the *Langham*, it was my grandfather who found him," said Captain Pete as they all sat down. He pulled a piece of driftwood out of one pocket and a knife out of another one. Then he settled in to tell Sam and Becky the story of what happened so many years ago.

"As it turns out," continued Captain Pete, "young Tom's mom and dad were dead. His father was a sailor who was lost at sea, and his poor mother died of a broken heart not long after. Tom was an orphan when he was only twelve years old.

"Tom lived with an uncle and aunt who didn't have any children and didn't want any. They treated Tom like a servant, making him do lots of heavy chores and barely feeding him. The uncle beat Tom if he did anything wrong and only let him go to school when all the chores were done.

"At school, Tom learned to read. He loved reading about other people and other places. When he read a book, he forgot about his horrible relatives—at least for a while.

"Tom's life was pretty miserable except when he was at school or down by the docks. At the docks he could watch the ships coming in and out of the harbor. He loved watching the sailors working on the ships and he promised himself that some day he would be on one of those ships.

"Tom's uncle was always angry and most of the time he took out his anger on Tom. One day, after an argument with a neighbor, the uncle was so angry that he hit Tom across the face and gave him a bloody nose."

Captain Pete stopped whittling for a minute and looked out over the water. "I just don't see how a grown man could hit a boy like that," he said. "It's just not right." He cleared his throat and, after a few minutes, started cutting at the wood in his hand again.

"Anyway, that was the day Tom decided to leave. He had a friend who lived near the docks, and this friend had an older brother who was a sailor on a ship called the *Langham*. The *Langham* was leaving that afternoon, and his friend's brother said if Tom could sneak onto the ship, he would help him hide.

"So that very day, Tom crept on board the *Langham* and became a stowaway. His friend's brother helped him hide from everyone else on the ship and brought him scraps of food to eat. Tom hid during the day and stretched his legs by walking around at night. It was a tough life for a twelve-year-old boy, but Tom was happier than he'd been since his mother died.

"My Grandpa Dave found Tom after about a week. He was as skinny as a rail and had bruises all over his body. Grandpa Dave knew right away that Tom had been beaten. He asked Tom why he was on the ship, but Tom wouldn't tell him anything— he was afraid that my Grandpa Dave would send him back to his uncle.

"Grandpa Dave finally convinced Tom that he wasn't going to send him back, so Tom told him the whole story. Grandpa Dave talked to the captain of the ship—Captain Sinclair—and the captain decided to let Tom stay on board.

"When Grandpa Dave told him he could stay, Tom was so happy he almost cried. Grandpa Dave told us he saw Tom wiping tears from his eyes.

"So, Tom became a cabin boy on the *Langham*. He was very smart and worked hard. All the crew liked him, and they were often surprised to find the ship's deck already mopped or tangles of rope coiled neatly on the deck.

"Tom loved being on the *Langham* and helping the sailors, but he was still a stowaway, which was technically a **crime**. If he left the ship, Tom could be arrested. So, when the other sailors went ashore, Tom stayed on the *Langham*.

CRIME ✳
(crym)
An illegal act. Something done that is against the law.

Everyone on the ship kept Tom's secret so he wouldn't be sent back to his uncle.

"Late in October in 1910, on a trip up to Port Arthur, the *Langham* was crossing Lake Superior when a huge storm came up. The Captain decided to take shelter from the storm right here in Bete Grise Bay."

Captain Pete's whittling had turned the driftwood into a bird, but now he stood up and put the knife and the driftwood bird in his pocket. He looked at Sam and Becky and said in a hushed voice, "That's when something worse than a storm got hold of the *Langham*."

Chapter 13
MALINA

Becky had held her breath throughout Captain Pete's story, but now she spoke.

"Malina! Is that when the mean witch Malina put the curse on Tom? Is that when she burned the ship?"

"Well of course we don't know for sure—since Malina doesn't admit to anything—but on the night that the *Langham* sheltered in Bete Grise Bay, Captain Sinclair told my grandfather about a witch who was mad at him. This witch was in love with Captain Sinclair but he was in love with

✳ **FURIOUS**
(FYUR-e-ous)
Very, very angry.

someone else. When he told the witch that he could never love her, it made her **furious**.

"Now, for some time, the sailors had seen strange things out on the lake. There was lightning in a clear night sky, swirling mists that never lifted, and sunsets that looked liked fire—even in the thick fog. I think all of these things had to do with Malina's great anger at the captain.

"Finally Malina decided to punish Captain Sinclair by destroying his beloved ship. She started the fire when the crew was on shore so no one could see her. When she realized that Tom was still on board and had seen her start the fire, she put a curse on him so he couldn't tell anyone.

"That night, the *Langham* burned down to the water, and then sank. All the crew were ashore when the ship caught fire—at least all of the *official* crew. Captain Sinclair and my grandfather looked all over for Tom on the shore. When they realized that Tom must have been on the ship when it burned, they were stunned and very sad. There was an investigation into the fire, but the official cause remains 'unknown.'"

Everyone was quiet for a few minutes after Captain Pete finished his story. They were all thinking about the boy who died in the fire and became a ghost.

"Captain Pete," asked Becky softly, "who was Captain Sinclair in love with?"

"Malina's twin sister, Marina."

* * * * *

"So, that's the whole story," said Captain Pete sighing a very deep sigh. "Poor Tom died and was cursed because Malina was jealous of her sister."

"And if we don't figure out the last clue, she's going to curse him all over again," said Sam.

"Hey, Captain Pete, we met a lady on the beach who said you gave her a good-luck medallion."

"You mean the one with the picture of the Mendota Lighthouse on it?"

"That's the one!" said Sam. "Do you know what it said on the back?"

"I remember there was something etched on the back, but I never read it. It was too small for these old eyes to read. When I gave it to her, she said she'd polish it so we could see what it said."

"Well, it's gone now," said Becky. "Lost. She put it on Spot's collar as a good-luck charm and somehow it got lost when her sister took Spot for a walk."

Captain Pete shook his head. "Marina shouldn't have let Spot go for a walk with that medallion. He's too rough."

"Marina?" exclaimed Sam. "So, the lady on the beach with the dog is Marina?"

"That makes sense," said Becky. "So, that means that the sister who took Spot for a walk is..."

"Malina," said Sam softly.

"Malina," echoed Captain Pete. "And if Malina's done something with that medallion... it's gone."

A Michigan Lighthouse Adventure

Chapter 14
FINDERS KEEPERS

Suddenly there was a lot of splashing in the water beside the boat.

"That's the divers," said Captain Pete. "I was thinking that it was about time for them to come back up."

Sam and Becky watched as the divers surfaced and helped each other climb the ladder into the boat. They all wore wet suits to protect them from the cold water of Lake Superior, and they all had air tanks, masks, and fins. The last diver up was the dive leader, Angus. He handed his big flashlight up to Captain Pete and then heaved himself up the ladder.

"Thanks Cap'n," said Angus as Captain Pete gave him a hand into the boat. "Here, I brought you something. I just found it. I know it's illegal to remove anything from a shipwreck, but I know this doesn't belong to the wreck. You can tell it's only been down there a day or two. I thought you'd like it as a souvenir. I know how fond you are of Bete Grise Bay and the Mendota light."

AFT
(aft)
The back end of a boat. The opposite of forward.

"Somebody must have lost this pretty recently," said Angus. "It hasn't been corroded by the water at all. It was just sitting there on the **aft** anchor."

Angus opened his gloved hand and there, in the middle, was a brassy gold medallion. An engraving of the Mendota Lighthouse was clearly etched on it.

Sam and Becky watched as Captain Pete examined the medallion closely.

"I don't believe it," he said. "It can't be."

"What, Captain Pete? What is it?"

"This is the same medallion I gave to Marina. See, it's got the Mendota Lighthouse. I can't believe you found it on the shipwreck."

"There's something written on the back of it," Angus said as he pulled off his swim fins, "but it was too dark down there for me to make it out. Can you read it Cap'n?"

"What does the writing say, Captain Pete?" said Becky. "Can you read it?

103

Slowly—for his eyes were old and the writing was very small—Captain Pete read these words from the back of the medallion:

Iron bars cannot hold me,
Nor chains of greatest length,
I burst through walls of solid glass,
But water splits my strength.

I can help the weak to see,
Or make a strong man blind,
Darkness dies when I appear,
And treasures you can find.

What am I?

"It's the riddle," whispered Becky.

"Now all we have to do is solve it," said Sam.

Chapter 15
DINNER, ANYONE?

"Ahoy there, Captain! Hey, I thought you guys were going to catch up with us." Mom and Dad paddled up to the side of the diving boat.

"We got the picture!" Mom held up the digital camera triumphantly.

"It wasn't easy," confided Dad, "especially when your mother wanted to stand up to get a better angle. But we managed to get a wonderful picture of the lighthouse and the entrance to the canal. I think there's even a hawk flying across the sky at just the right time."

"Captain Pete," called Mom, "Mike and I want to ask you to dinner tonight. It's our last night in the area and we want to say thank you for all the help you've been. I know the kids would love it too."

"That's a great idea, Mom," said Sam. "How about it, Captain Pete? Will you come eat dinner with us tonight?"

"I'd be honored," said the Captain. "Thank you kindly."

"Why don't you come over around seven?" said Mom. "There'll be plenty of time after dinner for a walk on the beach. I think there's a full moon tonight, so it should be lovely. Do you know where we're staying?"

"It's the old Bailey place isn't it? Right on the bay?"

"That's the one," said Dad. "OK, kids let's get going. We have a lot of things to finish up today."

"You're so right, Dad," said Sam.

"Here, Becky," said Captain Pete holding out his hand. "You and Sam take this. I think it would make a nice souvenir of your trip to the Keweenaw."

"Thanks, Captain Pete," said Becky as she carefully took the medallion from his hand. "We'll take good care of it."

"See you tonight, Captain," said Dad as he put his paddle back in the water. "Now Alice, let's do this together, remember?"

"I do, Mike, but wouldn't it be better to go this way?"

Sam shook his head as he watched Mom and Dad zigzag across the bay. "It's a miracle they ever get anywhere," he said. He climbed into the kayak after Becky was settled and called, "We'll see you tonight, Captain Pete."

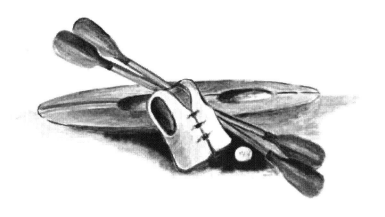

Chapter 16
SEEING THE LIGHT

Sam and Becky followed Mom and Dad back to the shore. They pulled their kayak from the water and looked up as Mom called to them.

"Would you guys put the life vests away, and then carry your kayak up and put it in the garage? Your Dad and I are going to town to get food for dinner. Sam, would you make one of your kitchen sink salads? And Becky, will you wash the blueberries and help Sam with the salad? We'll make dessert when I get back."

"OK, Mom," said Sam.

"Sure, Mom," called Becky. "Will you get some ice cream to go with dessert?"

"Already on my list," replied Mom. "You two behave. We should be back in about an hour."

Sam and Becky waved as Dad pulled the car onto the main road. "This is good," said Sam picking up his end of the kayak. "Now we have some time to figure out that riddle. We should be getting pretty good at solving these by now."

"Yeah," said Becky, picking up the other end of the kayak and walking backwards toward the garage, "but these riddles usually have a catch to them. You know, a trick or a play on words or something like that. So, we have to read the riddle again and read the words exactly."

When they were in the garage, Sam gently set down his end of the kayak. "OK," he said, "read it again."

Becky set down the other end of the kayak and pulled the medallion from her pocket. "I can't see it," she said, "it's too dark in here. Let's go outside."

When she stepped outside into the sunlight, she quickly shut her eyes. "Oww!" she cried, putting her hand over her eyes, "Now I can't see anything—it's too bright!"

"Just come back in here," said Sam. "We can open the shutters and let the light in through the windows. Can you see now?"

"Yeah, I'm fine. It's just when I went out of the dark into the bright light so fast. It blinded me. I can see now. OK, here's the riddle." And she slowly read the back of the medallion again.

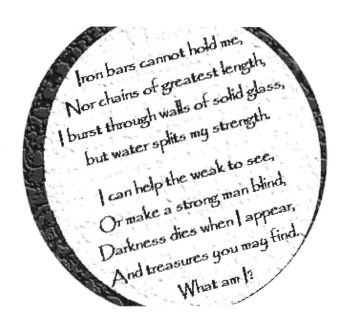

Iron bars cannot hold me,
Nor chains of greatest length,
I burst through walls of solid glass,
but water splits my strength.

I can help the weak to see,
Or make a strong man blind,
Darkness dies when I appear,
And treasures you may find.
What am I?

"I know the answer's close," said Sam. "it's just that I can't put it all together."

Suddenly a clap of thunder rumbled from across the lake. "C'mon," said Becky, "let's get our life vests before it starts to rain." They ran back to the edge of the water and grabbed the life vests and paddles just as the rain started pouring down.

"It's a good thing we're already wet," said Sam, "cause if we weren't, we would be now!"

"I know," said Becky, "I'm soaked. We'd better get inside and get that salad done. Maybe if we don't think about the riddle for a little while, the answer will come to us."

*****

By the time Becky had changed into dry clothes, Sam was already in the kitchen. His clothes were dry, but his hair was still wet. He was squatting in front of the refrigerator with a frown on his face.

"There's not much here, Becky," he said as she joined him.

"I thought that was the whole point of a kitchen sink salad," said Becky reaching over his head to get the bag of blueberries sitting on the top shelf. "That you can put anything in it."

"Yeah, but you have to start with something," growled Sam.

"There are some apples over there on the table if you want them."

Sam poked his head up and looked over at the apples. "That's a good start," he said, smiling. "Hey, look! It stopped raining! There should be a great rainbow somewhere."

"Let's go see if we can find it."

They went outside and looked up at the dark clouds moving quickly away and the patches of blue sky starting to appear.

"The rainbow should be opposite the sun," said Sam as he scanned the sky. "The rain water splits the light from the sun into a spectrum of colored light and makes a rainbow."

"Yeah, Sam, I know. I got an 'A' in science, remember? You don't have to—wait a minute! Say what you just said again—just like you said it before."

"You mean the part about the water splitting the light into a rainbow?"

Becky pulled the medallion from her pocket and read out loud, "'But water splits my strength.' Sam, do you think..."

"...that 'light' is the answer? Let's try it. Iron bars can't hold light. It goes right through them. Same thing with chains—they can't stop light."

"And light can go through solid glass—no problem," said Becky.

"Light helps you see, but it can also blind you just like it did to you when you went out into the sunlight after being in the dark garage."

"When you turn on a light, darkness goes away, or dies, and you can find lost treasures."

"Becky, we found the answer to the riddle!"

Chapter 17
AN AFTER-DINNER WALK

Dinner was delicious. Dad grilled fresh lake trout wrapped in bacon and Mom fixed her special garlic fries. There was Sam's "kitchen sink" salad, and Mom and Becky had made dessert using the wild blueberries they picked yesterday.

Captain Pete was right on time. Hee brought a bouquet of Keweenaw wildflowers for Mom and some fresh smoked **whitefish** with crackers to share with everyone.

WHITEFISH ✳
(WHITE-fish)
A delicious fresh-water fish that lives in cold waters.

"Where did you get this whitefish, Captain Pete?" asked Dad. "It's smoked to perfection. Someone really knows how to do it right."

"Well, thank you, sir. I've been working on it for about twenty years. It's about time I got it right."

⚓ GRUNT
(grunt)
A dessert made with cooked fruit (in this case blueberries), topped with dumplings made from flour, sugar, milk, and butter, and steamed until done. Top it with whipped cream or ice cream. (Yum!) The name grunt comes from the noise the fruit makes as it cooks.

"You made this? Honestly, Captain Pete, I've never put anything so good in my mouth. Mmmm."

After dinner, Becky served the dessert. "It's Grandma Anne's famous blueberry **grunt**," she told them. "I used the wild blueberries we picked yesterday. Just wait 'til you taste it—especially with a little scoop of Vanilla Bean ice cream on top." said Becky.

"It *does* taste good," said Dad after his first bite, "but I have to tell you, the name is a little gross. I mean, blueberry grunt? I think we need to work on a new image for that poor dessert."

"Well, no matter what it's called," said Captain Pete, "it's delicious. But I think I ate too much of it."

"Kids, why don't you take Captain Pete to the beach and let him walk off some of his dinner? Dad and I will clean up the dishes. You two have been a big help today."

"Thanks, Mom! Come on, Captain Pete. Let's go take a walk on the singing sands."

"Oh, so you've heard the story about the sad Indian maiden?" asked the captain as he, Sam, and Becky walked toward the beach.

"What story?" asked Becky, "We just know that the sand sings to you when you walk on it."

"Spot thinks it's barking at him," laughed Sam recalling Spot's crazy attempts to attack the sand.

"Well," said Captain Pete, "according to the story, a young Native American maiden lost her true love to the sea and is singing until he returns. The sand sings only on this beach, where the maiden calls for her love. If you take the sand somewhere else, it's quiet. It's a mystery why it sings here and nowhere else."

"I know another mystery," said Becky, "and maybe an answer. We've been working on the last riddle, Captain Pete, and we think we solved it."

"That's great!" said Captain Pete. "Read the riddle again, and then tell me the answer you came up with. I can't wait!"

"Me, either," said a voice behind them.

"Tom! I was wondering where you were. Becky and I think we know the answer to the riddle!"

"I knew you could do it!" said Tom whose whole body was visible now. "Go on, Sam. Read the riddle. We'll see if you and Becky have the right answer."

So, Sam read the riddle again. When he got to the end he looked at Becky and together they said, "The answer to the riddle is 'light.'"

Chapter 18
IN THE SHADOW OF THIS TOWER

After Sam and Becky said the answer to the riddle, nobody spoke. Even the waves and the wind seemed to hold their breath.

And then, a gray, ghostly glow appeared over the place where the *Langham* lay in Bete Grise Bay. It grew brighter and brighter until it reached Sam, Becky, Tom, and Captain Pete on the beach. And, in the bright light, they realized they were no longer alone.

The light had brought two women to the beach. They looked exactly alike, except that one woman was smiling and one was frowning.

The frowning woman took a step toward Tom. She narrowed her eyes as she looked at him, and said, "So, you did it. You solved the riddles. You beat me…at least this time. Very well, then."

And before anyone could say anything else, she turned toward the Mendota Lighthouse and lifted her arms. The light that flashed in the tower went dark as Malina spoke these words:

In the shadow of this tower,
In the lateness of this hour,
Return his gifts, his form, and voice,
His special knowledge, his gift of choice.

From now until eternity,
Remove the curse and set him free.
Give back to him his magic power,
Hear my voice, oh magic tower.

As Malina finished, the lighthouse tower glowed, and then its guiding light started to flash again. For a moment, Tom seemed to absorb the light, and then the glow slowly disappeared. The sky returned to its darkness and the full moon shone on the water making a silver path on the bay.

Malina watched the glowing light fade from the lighthouse. "It's done," she said looking at Tom. And then, with no warning, she turned herself into a beautiful black seagull. She "cawed" once to Marina, and then flew gracefully away along the moon path and out of sight.

"How do you feel, Tom?" asked Marina.

"I feel good," said Tom. "I can talk, you can see me, and…wait a minute, there's a ship that's in trouble. I can feel it! And the best part is—I can help!"

"I'm glad you figured out the riddles, Tom," said Marina, "and I'm glad that you'll be able to help the sailors again. They've missed you."

"I don't know what to say. I owe it all to Sam and Becky and, of course, to you too, Captain Pete."

"Don't forget Marina," said Captain Pete.

"Yes, thank you, Marina," said Tom. "Thank you for helping us even when we didn't know you were helping. We couldn't have done it without you."

Tom took a step back from the group. "I'm not going to say good bye," he said, "because I just know we'll see each other again. But now I'm going to go help those sailors." He turned to leave, but at the last second, he looked back at Sam and Becky and said softly, "Thank you."

And, then, as they watched, Tom faded gently into the night.

****

"I guess I'll be on my way too," said Marina.

"Marina, can I ask you a question before you go?" asked Sam.

"Certainly," said Marina. "What do you want to know?"

"Why is Malina so mean?"

"Oh, Sam, I don't think she's really mean—at least she didn't used to be. It's just that she's so terribly unhappy. We were always best friends until…. Well, she's still my sister, so I have to keep trying to help her. She's so full of anger and she holds on to it so tightly. That's what makes her do such mean things."

"Marina," asked Becky softly, "is Malina angry because Captain Sinclair loved you and not her?"

Marina sighed. "Yes. John—Captain Sinclair—and I have been in love since we first met. When Malina met him, she thought—since we were twins—he could just as easily love her as me. She tried to trick him and take him from me, but true love can't be fooled.

※ **RENDEZVOUS**
(RON-day-voo)
A meeting that takes place at a specific time and place.

"Now, I have to go. I have a **rendezvous** with a special captain. We're going dancing! Pete, will you do me a favor and take care of Spot?"

"Of course I will, Marina. You know if you ever need anything...."

Marina smiled at Captain Pete, raised a hand in farewell to the others, and then turned and walked into the glow of the shipwrecked *Langham*.

As the others watched, the glowing light grew brighter for just a few minutes and then rose higher and higher until it became part of the dazzling Northern Lights dancing over Bete Grise Bay.

Chapter 19
A NEW BEGINNING

When Sam, Becky, and Captain Pete arrived back at the cabin, they found Mom and Dad entertaining a new visitor—Spot!

Dad was down on all fours on the living room rug barking at Spot. Spot was crouched down with his tail up in the air, and he was growling back at Dad.

Mom was sitting by the window seat that looked out onto the bay. "Where have you been?" she called as they walked into the room. "Did you see all of those strange lights over the bay? It must have been some sort of Northern Lights event. It was amazing!"

"Where did Spot come from?" asked Sam.

"Is that his name?" said Dad sitting back on his knees like a good dog. "We heard a scratching at the door and, when we opened it, we were attacked by this ferocious, furry monster."

Captain Pete chuckled. "A friend left him here for me to take care of for a while. Thank you for doggie-sitting!"

"No problem," said Dad brushing the dog hair off his pants as he stood up. "So, where have you guys been? That was some walk you took."

"Well," said Becky looking at Sam, "we were working on some riddles."

"I *love* riddles," said Dad. "Did you solve it? Can I help?"

"Well actually, Dad," Sam said with a grin, "we did solve it. And, you already helped us by taking us to find moose tracks in Copper Harbor."

The End

Just So You Know...

Remember I said there were lots of great books to read and websites to visit? Well, here are some of my favorites.

Books to Read

Hivert-Carthew, Annick and Martha M. Diebboli. *Ghostly Lights: Great Lakes Lighthouse Tales of Terror.* Manchester, MI: Wilderness Adventure Books, 1999.

House, Katherine L. *Lighthouses for Kids.* Chicago: Chicago Review Press, Inc., 2008.

Rylant, Cynthia. *The Eagle (The Lighthouse Family).* New York: Simon & Schuster Books for Young Readers, 2004.

Websites to Visit

"Bete Grise Bay (Mendota), Mi." *Lighthouse Friends.com.* <www.lighthousefriends.com/light.asp?ID=227>.

"First Woman Lightkeeper on the Keweenaw Peninsula." *Lighthouse Depot, Lighthouse Digest.* <www.lighthousedepot.com/lite_digest.asp?action=get_article&sk=1254>.

"Langham." *Great Lakes Diving.* <www.divethegreatlakes.com/search/wreckDive.php?id=2336>.

"Langham." *Keweenaw Underwater Preserve.* <www.ship-wrecks.net/shipwreck/keweenaw/langham.html>.

"Mendota Light and Canal." *Hunt's Guide to Michigan's Upper Peninsula.* <www.hunts-upguide.com/lac_la_belle_mendota_light_and_canal.html.

Read *all* of the
Michigan Lighthouse Adventures
and join Sam and Becky
as they
solve mysteries on
Michigan's Upper Peninsula!

THE CLUE AT
COPPER HARBOR

THE MYSTERY AT
EAGLE HARBOR

THE SECRET OF
BETE GRISE BAY